Cornering the Cowgirl

Covet the Cowboy Series, Episode 2

An Erotic Short Story
By

Katie O'Connor

Cornering the Cowgirl

Covet the Cowboy Series, Episode 2

Dedication

This one is for the love of my life. Hubby, thanks for your patience and encouragement, even if you insist on referring to this story as Humping the Heifer. Love you, old guy.
It's also for my favorite fan, Samantha. She's a reader, a critic and a support network unto herself. She's been along for the ride since my first book. I wouldn't be as far along in my career as I am without her. Thanks, Doll. Someday, we'll meet in person!

Visiting the Ranch

Alex Kirk pulled into a roadside turnout and slowed her Honda Civic to a stop. Her GPS indicated that she had another three miles to her destination, the Joe Brooks Cattle Company.

Her stomach roiled and her hands shook, this was such an enormous mistake. What the hell was she thinking? She'd shared one super hot night with Joe nearly two months ago, and here she was chasing him down. He'd think she was crazy, sleazy, or both, if he didn't already.

The morning after their incredible encounter, she'd found his business card in her pocket and had no idea when he'd put it there. She tossed it in the trash, took it out, tore it in half, threw it away, and after some serious thought, taped it back together and pinned it to her bulletin board. Indecision wasn't typical. She knew that they'd had a one-off, but something wouldn't let her destroy her only potential contact for him. Now, after months of the tattered card mocking her every time she passed it, she'd given in to its taunting to seek him out.

It whispered to her from the passenger seat, she glanced at it: its tattered edges glared defiantly back at her. Four simple words, an address, and a phone number seemed to indicate he was telling the truth about his name. Okay, maybe it didn't prove anything; anybody could get business cards printed. But it certainly improved his credibility. Her internet research told her that the company did exist. But niggling doubts said anyone could have found the card and passed it on. Hell, one of the ranch employees may have had the card to give out to potential clients. There was no concrete proof the man she'd entangled herself with was actually Joe Brooks, but she sure hoped he was. Why else would he have snuck the card into her pocket?

Her face flushed thinking of what she'd done…no, what *they'd* done that night. She didn't know him, he was a complete stranger she'd bumped into and hooked up with. She'd never had sex with a stranger before Joe. Hell, she usually dated a man half a dozen times before letting him kiss her goodnight; and sex came several dates after that. She didn't know if it was the beer, the atmosphere, or Joe himself that made her shed her inhibitions like a debutante shedding her fur coat mid-July. But she had. And wow!

Holy wow!

She'd run into him, literally, in the beer garden, and they'd seduced each other. He'd been so sexy and so attractive. He'd introduced himself as Joe Brooks and his self confidence and humor had been infectious. They'd shared two wickedly satisfying rounds of sex, one in a taxi! They might have gone another round, but he was sharing his hotel room and there was no way in hell she'd take a stranger to her place. Instead, they'd ended up at Gina's Café for coffee and pie and had talked for hours. They had a lot of common interests, and where they disagreed, it wasn't uncomfortable. By the end of the long evening, she felt like she'd known him forever.

After that encounter, Joe probably thought she slept with anyone. Heat scorched in her face. Good grief, she'd practically raped him. Twice. She wasn't usually like that, but he'd had her fired up. Big time. Her best friend Janine had chalked it up to love at first sight, plain and simple. But then, Janine loved every cowboy she'd ever knocked boots with. Alex knew it was lust, plain and simple. A biological urge to procreate and nothing more. So why couldn't she stop thinking about him?

Finding that card in her pocket was both intriguing and scary. She'd chalked the evening up to a chance encounter, a sexy hot chance encounter. But, did he want her to contact him? Okay, stupid question. If he'd wanted their encounter to remain anonymous, he certainly wouldn't have slipped the card into the pocket of her skirt. The only conclusion she could draw was that he wanted her to contact him. He had no way to find her. She hadn't divulged her last name and all he knew about her career was that she was an office manager. In a city this size, office managers were a dime a dozen so he'd never find her that way.

But slipping the card in her pocket? Why all the cloak and dagger?

She banged a fist on the steering wheel. She should have called first. This could turn out to be such a disaster. She slipped the car into drive and cautiously pulled back onto the highway. Nothing ventured, nothing gained, and she'd already driven two hours outside the city. She might as well carry through her half-baked idea of showing up unannounced. Coming here was crazy, but she wasn't stupid. Janine knew where she was headed and when she planned to come home. No sense turning a risky situation into blatant stupidity. If she didn't report in, help would come looking for her.

So here she was, in search of the hottest, dreamiest, sexiest hunk she'd ever laid eyes and hands on. Seeing him again might be the only way she'd purge him from her brain and her fantasies.

Arriving at the ranch way too soon for her peace of mind, she turned onto a narrow, paved road, or was it a driveway? Pristine, white pole fences lined the road on both sides. The ditches were mowed and neat. Cattle ranged the fields behind the fences for as far as she could see. They'd chewed the grass short enough that it looked like an expanse of lawn. In the distance, the fields morphed into mixed arboreal forest with towering poplars and solid pine and spruce. In front of her an impressive wrought iron sign, suspended from two enormous wooden posts, arched across the road and announced that she'd arrived at the Joe Brooks Cattle Company. She pulled to the side, stopped, and stared. She'd expected a farm, maybe a ranch. This place seemed colossal and not at all what she'd been expecting.

Further up the lane, she could see oversized metal buildings, at least four red steel barns, rows and rows of livestock pens, and a gigantic house. Who lived in a house that big?

Oh yeah, this had been a superb mistake. Time to cut and run and forget she'd ever been here. There wasn't room to easily turn around on the road. Rather than make an eight-point turn, she drove ahead seeking a safe place to change directions. She turned onto a gravel lane that ended at a small red and white building that looked like an oversized shed. She'd be able to back out and turn around here.

Joe stood to the side of the feed shed watching a small green Honda sneak up his driveway. Whoever it was must be lost. They paused outside the main gate to look around before creeping forward and turning into the roadway to stop twenty feet from where he stood in the shed's shadows. Something about the action struck him as strange. They must be up to no-good. Why else would they stop here, and not up at the house or barns?

The driver's head pivoted revealing waves of long blonde hair.

No way! Alex hadn't finally shown up, had she?

He had to be hallucinating. He'd been dreaming of that hair for months and he couldn't shake the memories of their first and only encounter. They'd clicked sexually and personally. He'd given up hope of ever seeing her again. He'd even considered taking out a personal ad to find her. His mind must be playing tricks on him.

He stepped out from the shadows and called out, "Hi there, can I help you?"

The blonde whipped her head around to face him. The sun visor concealed half of her face, and he couldn't be certain, but it sure looked like her.

Anticipation stirring, he strode toward the car. The door opened slowly, but the occupant didn't get out. Interesting. Half a dozen quick strides had him beside the car, leaning on top of the open door. The woman looked up at him, shading her eyes from the sun streaming behind him. He must look like a dark blob in a sky of bright light.

"Can you step back?" Her voice was strong, underlaid with a barely detectible tremble and she made a shooing motion with one hand. "I'll just turn around and go. I was lost and looking for a place to turn around."

It *was* her; he knew that sexy voice. He'd been hearing it in his erotic dreams for weeks. He'd had more than one wet awakening in the middle of the night. His late-night fantasies were turning him back into a lusty teenager. His cock hardened in response to the memories flashing through his mind: Ferris wheel, behind a fair booth, in a taxi. Damn. He almost groaned aloud.

"Don't run away now Just-Alex. You've only arrived. I'd about given up hope."

"Joe?" Hesitation made her voice tremble.

His cock stirred again. Damn, he loved the sound of his name on her lips. It slid down his body like warm whiskey with a wave of anticipation and arousal. Good lord, he was in trouble if her voice was wreaking this much havoc.

She inched out of the car and slid back along its side until she was three long strides away, out of his reach. Her beautiful green eyes flashed in the bright sunshine. Her gaze darted around looking everywhere but directly at him. Ah, so she was cautious and uncertain. Weirdly, that was a point in her favour. She'd must've waited so long to come because she didn't quite trust him, and who would trust a stranger after one quick encounter? Being here was a risk for her on more than one level. He admired her courage for taking the risk, though part of him wanted to chide her for doing so. Women needed to be cautious of strangers. He almost laughed at the contradicting thoughts. Arousal and protective instinct were two strange bedfellows.

"So," he drawled, "Would you like to drive up to the house and meet some of my hands? Get some feedback on who I am? I can follow you."

She swallowed hard and nodded. "Yes, please."

He chuckled. "I don't blame you one bit. But can you at least look at me? Maybe spare me a smile. God, I remember your smile and your laugh." He kept his voice light and teasing. Safe, with a hint of sexual innuendo thrown in. She was as skittish as a newborn colt.

She looked up at him and their eyes met. She blinked shyly and her gaze shifted to his shoulder. Timid little thing in the bright light of day. She'd lost the freedom that Buffalo Days and a couple beers had given her. Neither of them had been drunk, just relaxed and uninhibited. He'd never take advantage of a woman who didn't have her full faculties about her.

Now, he'd love another chance at her luscious body, but her caution was probably for the best. He wouldn't start anything unless she was all-in. He wanted more than a drunken encounter in the dark. He studied her from the tip of the red-painted toenails peeking out from her sexy high-heeled sandals, to the top of her shimmering blonde waves. His gaze was caught once or twice on the way up. First by those long, sexy legs; damn, they went on forever. They'd look incredible wrapped around his waist. Then by the naked skin of her belly and the generous swell of her breasts as they peeked out from behind her enticingly snug T-shirt. She was dressed for the heat of the afternoon, but damn, she was all curves and sex appeal. He had a notion that she'd turn him on dressed in a feed sack.

Blood thundered in his veins, his pulse pounded in his ears. He bunched his hands into fists to keep from taking her right there on the trunk of her car. That body should be illegal. He forced his arms and hands to relax and looked her in the eye. This time, she smiled and met his gaze.

"Come on, city girl. Get back in the car and drive up to the house. Park anywhere. I'll be up in a minute. I'll finish up here and hop on my quad. If anyone questions you, tell them you're waiting for me."

He stepped toward her. "I *am* glad you came." He reached up and wrapped a single strand of golden-blonde hair around one finger. "So soft." He released the strand and stepped back. "Go on now. I'll be right up."

He half expected her to disappear out of the yard and head back to the city. To his surprise, she turned the car toward the house. He didn't move until she was five hundred yards down the road.

Damn. His heart was still pounding and he couldn't wait to get another taste of her lips. Memories were good, but he knew damn well that reality was much, much better. Whistling, he finished setting out a fresh salt block, locked the building, and hopped on the quad.

Alex paced circles on the driveway in front of Joe's massive two-story house. Pristine white, it had forest green railings and shutters. She'd parked fifteen feet short of its enormous wrap-around porch. By the look of things, the covered veranda went at least three quarters of the way around the house. Brimming pots of flowers were placed with careful randomness between Adirondack chairs and double-wide swings. It'd be a lovely place to cozy up to read, watch the sunrise, or make love as the sun set. She clamped the reins on that thought. That wasn't why she was here.

Yeah, right. She laughed aloud at her own evasion of the truth. She couldn't get Joe, his sexy body, or his lovemaking out of her mind. She felt like a junkie Jones-ing for a hit. She'd been half hoping that he wasn't as good looking as her memory insisted.

But when he'd stepped out from behind that shed, she'd hit full arousal in seconds. Those long powerful legs, the tight T-shirt straining across his chest and over his biceps, and that tan cowboy hat…jeepers, a girl didn't stand a chance. Every woman from nine to ninety would want to tangle with Joe Brooks.

A door closed and she turned toward the house where a tall, grey-haired woman in a denim dress and floral apron had stepped out onto the porch. The woman waved and smiled brightly. "Can I help you, Miss?"

"Um. Hi. I'm just waiting for Joe. He said he'd be right up." The sound of a quad coming closer proved her words. "That must be him now." She waved toward the sound.

He brought the quad to a stop, hit the kill switch, and hopped off. "Here I am, as promised."

"Joseph, aren't you going to introduce me to your friend?" The woman chided lightly.

"Ma, this is Alex. Alex, this is my mother, Leticia Brooks."

"Call me Letty, dear." She stepped off the porch and offered her hand. "My son has atrocious manners, you'll have to forgive him."

"Hi, I'm Alex Kirk. Pleased to meet you." They shook hands. Letty had a shrewd look in her eye. Alex swallowed hard and tried not to flinch from the knowing, parental expression on her face. At length, Letty nodded and smiled, sending relief coursing through Alex's body, although she wasn't sure why she needed his mother's approval.

"Well, my cookies will be about done. I'll make fresh coffee. You come in for coffee and cookies, and I won't take no for an answer." Ten seconds later she was gone, screen door closing gently in her wake.

"Well, that confirms your name *is* Joe Brooks."

"You doubted me?" He clutched his hands over his chest, feigning mortal injury. "And you Just-Alex are Alex Kirk." He offered his hand. "I'm pleased to formally meet you."

Alex accepted the shake and squeaked in surprise when he tugged her forward into his embrace. He tipped his hat up and grinned down at her before wrapping both arms around her.

"Sorry, I can't wait any longer." Joe whispered.

He paused, allowing her a second to stop him. His lips skimmed across hers. Lightly at first and then with speed that left her breathless, he deepened the kiss, his tongue thrusting into her mouth, demanding she respond. Lust slammed through her. How the hell did one kiss do that? Three seconds of lip-lock and she was ready for him. Right here, right now.

Her arms slipped around his neck, her fingers searching for purchase in his hair, knocking his hat to the ground. Her left hand yanked on his neckline, dragging him closer as she kissed him back. He stepped toward her, inching her backward until she bumped up against her car. His arousal pressed against her belly, her knees went weak and she moaned. Her hips thrust forward, trying to get closer.

His arms came up, his hands buried in her hair. He leaned back. "I love your hair." His grip tightened and he tipped her head to the right and kissed her again. His lips trailed away from her mouth, across her cheek, he paused to nibble her ear before kissing his way down her neck to the neckline of her shirt.

She whimpered something inarticulate and clutched at his back.

A shrill wolf whistle jerked her back to reality. She pushed on his chest hoping to move him away.

He barely broke their kiss to call out. "Bro, you're fired if this isn't life or death."

He leaned back in and nuzzled her neck. "Damn, you taste intoxicating; like honey, vanilla, salt, and woman." He growled and trailed his tongue up to her ear. His breath was hot and electric. "Sorry, wrong place, wrong time. Right woman. Sorry, Alex, I have to see what he needs."

She nodded mutely, unable to form words. Passion and chagrin battled for supremacy. What was she doing, kissing him like that, right here in his front yard? Geez, his mother was inside the house. There could be dozens of people around and she'd have let him take her, right here on the driveway. She was losing it, all because of one kiss.

Joe stepped to the side and slid one arm around her waist. He turned toward the man standing on the grass twenty feet from them. He could have been Joe's twin. "So, what's up, James? And it better be critical. I was busy."

"Yeah, I caught that." His brother strode forward. "Aren't you going to introduce me to your date?"

"No, I'm not." He took a proprietary stance in front of her. "Ignore my idiot brother. He was just leaving."

"Nope. Just stopped by to say hi, and check out your lady friend." He reached around Joe to offer his hand. "I'm the good-looking brother. I'm James. Nice to meet you. When you're done with him, let me know. I'll show you how a real man acts. I'm not a pussy like him."

She shook his hand. No sparks. That was good, right? It proved her desires were specific to Joe, it wasn't just bizarre hormonal overload. "Nice to meet you, Joe."

"Come on, Alex." Joe grabbed his hat, climbed onto the quad, and patted the seat behind him. "Ignore my dipshit brother. I'll show you the horses before we grab some of Mom's cookies and tour the ranch."

Her tight, short skirt made it tricky, but she climbed up behind him and wrapped her arms around his waist. The seat was warm against her thighs, but not hot enough to burn. The quad rumbled to life with a tremor that echoed and enhanced the desire coursing through her. She wiggled a bit, grinding herself against the quad and against Joe's back. Might as well enjoy the ride. The trip to the barn was distressingly short, but entirely pleasant with the vibrations shifting through her body and lodging into her core.

Joe slid off the quad and offered his hand to help her dismount. She took it, despite not needing assistance. He yanked her close and leaned in to whisper. "Your face is flushed." He glanced down at her chest. "Your nipples are like rocks. Did you enjoy the ride?"

She blushed but nodded. "Nice vibration," she whispered back. "Too bad the ride was so short."

"Babe, we can go for a long ride later." His double meaning hit home with a fresh rush of panty-wetting arousal. "But first, a horse awaits." He took her hand and led her into the dark building. After a moment, her eyes adjusted to the dim lighting. Seven stalls lined each side of the stable. Half of them held horses and the rest were empty. It smelled of fresh hay with a hint of dust and manure. She breathed deeply; it reminded her of Buffalo Days and her visits to the barns to see the livestock. The dark, earthy scent relaxed her; tension she hadn't known she carried slipped away.

They walked from stall to stall, with Joe introducing each horse as they went by. "This is Bolton." He opened the stall door and led a filly out of the stall. "Pet her, like this."

Following Joe's lead, she offered her hand, knuckles turned under, for the filly to smell. Bolton head butted her and Alex laughed in delight. "She's lovely; but isn't Bolton an unusual name for a girl?"

"Don't even get me started on my mother and naming horses." His groan rumbled across her skin like a caress. Obviously, he loved his mother despite his half-hearted complaint.

They spent half an hour with the horses. Every time she shifted or moved, he was right beside her, touching her hand or trailing his fingers over her skin. She was on fire. Entering the barn, she'd assumed he was putting distance between them after his exuberant greeting. Now, she wasn't so sure. His casual touches were more seductive than a full-frontal attack. Damn, he was good. Too good. She was a mass of quivering arousal and they'd barely kissed.

With all the horses secure in their stalls, he led her outside and stopped beside the quad. "Got any real shoes? Those are sexy as hell, but not fit for quadding."

She wiggled her toes at him. "I do, but I like these."

"Very sexy, I'm trying not to take you right here. We'll be doing some walking; you need to cover up." He leaned in and kissed her before swatting her on the backside. "Hop on."

In seconds, they were back at her car. "Will I need pants?"

"Hell no! Change your shoes, I'll go get a snack to tide us over until dinner. You can stay for dinner, can't you?"

She nodded, slid off the quad, and sashayed over to the car. Opening the door, she bent low, letting her short skirt ride up, revealing even more of her legs. She twisted to reach into the back seat as if searching for something. Lifting one leg slightly, she shifted again, wondering if she was flashing a little of her pink lace panties.

"Damn, woman. You're killing me." The quad kicked into gear and he took off.

By the time he got back with a picnic basket tied to the front of the quad, she was waiting beside the car in her cowboy boots and hat, with a sweater in her hand. She'd locked her purse in the trunk. "Got a spot for my keys?" She asked, spinning around and patting her backside. "I don't have pockets in this skirt." She turned back toward him and ran her hands along her belly and thighs. "No pockets at all."

"Minx." He took the offered keys and slid them into his pocket.

She slipped into her sweater, leaving it open and climbed on behind him.

"Shame to cover up all that lovely skin." He shook his head sadly as they rolled forward.

It was impossible to keep her distance from him on a seat designed for one rider. She let herself slide forward against the heat of his back. The quad rumbled and vibrated beneath her and she spread her legs, wiggling her skirt higher and tipping her pelvis downward to better enjoy the sensation of the big machine vibrating against her core. If this turned into a long ride, she'd orgasm before they got there. Her breath hitched in her throat as an impending orgasm reared ever closer.

Abruptly, the quad stopped and shut off. Joe turned toward her. "Am I going too fast? Your breathing is off." The question was serious and in no way teasing.

"Hell no, you're not going nearly fast enough." She slid off the quad and looked around. They were separated from the yard by a thick row of trees; no one else was in sight. She yanked her skirt even higher and climbed in front of him straddling his lap. "Kiss me, again."

"You're killing me." He groaned and yanked her forward until her pussy was tight against his erection.

She ground into his hardness. "Aw, poor baby." She tipped her face up and ran her tongue across his lips. "I said kiss me, cowboy."

"Who am I to argue?" Suiting deed to words, he pulled her tighter, thrust up against her, and drove his tongue deep into her mouth. No questions, no apologies, just passion. She whimpered and kissed him back.

Joe couldn't believe his luck. First, he'd met her at Buffalo Days, and now after several weeks she'd shown up. Her passion wasn't an aberration caused by drink and frivolity. She seemed stone-cold sober and she was all over him. He was rock hard and damn near ready to take her without any foreplay. He'd never met a woman so quick to ignite. The logistics of having her right here, right now, on the quad, were difficult but by all that was holy he was going to try.

The harder he kissed, the harder she kissed back. He wrapped his hand in the luscious length of her hair and tugged her head back. She leaned away from him, exposing her neck and cleavage to his view. He trailed one finger from her ear, down her neck, and across the curve of her breasts where they threatened to pop out of her top.

"Wait," she groaned and wiggled free of his hand.

Disappointment rocked him. Had he pushed too hard, too fast? Had he misread her intentions?

In two quick moves, she discarded her sweater and T-shirt, tossing them carelessly onto the ground. She leaned back against the steering bar and let him look his fill. Her abdomen was both soft and flat, it begged to be tasted, but not nearly so much as the breasts that overflowed the pink lace bra that matched the panties she'd flashed him earlier.

"You going to look and drool all day or are you going to touch me?" Her voice was a teasing lilt. She slid her hands from the top of her skirt, up her body, and cupped her breasts.

His cock twitched under her. She smiled a naughty smile and pushed her breasts together, tipping her head forward to lick the tops of them with her tongue. "Mm. Delicious. You should taste them."

Somehow, he knew she didn't want him to move; she wanted to display herself to him. He could live with that. "I want to see them first."

She quirked an eyebrow at him and laughed. It was the most uninhibited sound he'd ever heard. "The sun feels so good on my skin." Her voice was almost a purr. She stretched long, raising her arms over her head and grinding against him.

She stroked her hands down her arms and onto her chest. She cupped her breasts, squeezing and releasing them, pushing them together and pulling them apart. She wiggled one arm out of her bra strap and then the other and pushed the offending garment down to her waist. Her nipples were dusty brown morsels, hard as rock, standing out from the golden tan of her skin. They strained for attention. He lost all power to resist and leaned forward, drawing one taut nipple into his mouth, pinching the other between thumb and forefinger. God, she was amazing.

He'd never known a woman as passionate as Alex. If he could, he'd freeze this moment and capture her expression. A nipple in each hand, he squeezed lightly, her mouth dropping open in a sexy O. Oh yeah. His cock twitched at the sight. Before the day was through, he'd be inside that mouth again.

Her nails dug into his forearms. Was he hurting her?

"Don't stop, that feels incredible."

Her breathless words sent a fresh rush of blood to his cock. Jesus, he was going to explode in his pants like a fucking teenager. Moisture seeped through his jeans. Hers? His? Joe couldn't be certain which. Damn, he needed her to be as ready as he was.

Alex pushed against him. Not to push him away, but to encourage him. She grasped his head in one hand and pulled him closer, thrusting up, shoving her breast further into his mouth. He started slow. Flicking and teasing her nipples, tasting and testing.

"Harder," she groaned.

"Like this?" He clenched her nipple lightly between his teeth.

"Yes. Harder." She ground against him. She was going to orgasm just from this. It was crazy, it was incredible. Her entire body was on fire for him. He inflamed her senses like no man ever had.

He bit down on her nipple, sucking and flicking it with his tongue while he lightly squeezed and twisted the other. "Yes. Please." She pushed against his cock, thrusting her hips up and down, grinding and twisting until it stroked against her clit perfectly. Thank God for skirts and miniscule panties. She was going to come. Right here. Right now. Grinding against Joe in the middle of a field, in the middle of the day, where anyone could interrupt them.

She bucked and writhed as he tortured her nipples; pulling and releasing, pinching and twisting. Her breathing came in gasps, her heartbeat thundered in her ears. Goosebumps erupted over her entire body. She gushed moisture and exploded into heaven.

She came back to earth slowly. He was kissing her breasts softly, tasting and exploring. She struggled to sit up, to embrace him.

"Relax. Take a second to breathe. I'll get mine. Later."

She flushed. She hadn't even considered his needs. Being with him drove her passion into overdrive until she could do nothing but take from him. She covered her eyes with one arm, hiding her chagrin.

"Relax, city girl." He pumped his hips, shoving his cock against her sensitive core. "You've got me wet right through my jeans. My cock can feel your wet heat." There was a tone, almost amazement, to his voice. "I want to be buried, balls deep, inside you. I want to feel your pussy clench around me, squeezing, milking and drawing out every drop."

She struggled upright, making him groan with the inadvertent contact with his cock. "I need you. Now. Inside me."

"That isn't going to be easy, not on a quad." He chuckled.

Yanking at his shirt, she pulled it free of his waistband and over his head. She tossed it on top of her own discarded clothing and leaned in to tongue his nipples. "Mm."

"Stop." The single word was more command than plea. "Get off me and pick up that clothing." He gestured to the discarded items. Something in his face told her he was serious, but not angry. His eyes twinkled. Was this a challenge, a test of some sort?

"Why?"

"Because I told you to."

"And if I don't want to?" She wondered where this was going. What was he up to?

He reached around her and lightly slapped her on the ass. Pleasure jolted through her. "Move it. If you want me to fuck you, you'll do what I say. Pick up the clothing and climb on behind me."

"Bossy, aren't you?"

He smacked her again, harder this time. Hard enough that it stung. She barely knew him; did she dare trust him? Doubt plagued her and she worried her lip with her teeth.

"Get off the quad and pick up the clothing. Please."

She studied his face. There was no malice. She felt no fear. This was a game, one she'd never played before. She wasn't certain she wanted to, but then she wasn't certain she didn't. She stared at him, pondering which way to go. In the end, she decided that enough people knew she was here that she was likely safe with him.

She hopped off and leaned in, pressing her open mouth against his cock. His jeans were soaked and he smelled like her arousal. She breathed deeply, enjoying the scent, and exhaled blowing hot air through his pants. He bucked against her. She backed away, turning her ass toward him, exposing herself to him, knowing the wet crotch of her panties was showing as she picked up the clothing and then climbed up behind him.

She pressed her naked chest against his bare back and reached around to squeeze his cock with one hand. "Let's go then. My pussy needs you."

Five minutes later, they pulled up alongside a mossy creek bank in an area shaded by tall pines. The shade was cool after the heat of the sun and felt glorious on her skin. Her nipples peaked at the change in temperature. Joe slid off the quad and stood there like a towering god, staring at her thoughtfully.

"I don't recall giving you permission to grab my dick."

"I don't recall asking," she sassed, unconcerned by his light chastisement.

"Sit on the quad and don't move until I come back." He unfastened the basket and headed toward the creek.

She immediately hopped off and shimmied out of her skirt and after a moment's thought, decided to leave her miniscule panties on. She leaned back against the seat and watched him spread out a blanket and open a bottle of wine.

He turned around, frowned and strode toward her, a teasing grin quirking his lips upward. "I told you to stay on the quad."

"My elbows are on the quad." Why she felt this crazy urge to push him, she didn't know.

"You're testing my patience," he warned and in one quick motion flipped her, face down, draped over the quad seat, arms dangling down the far side. "I think you need a lesson in obedience."

She froze, hanging in midair, her toes barely touching the ground, her ass exposed to him with nothing but a thin layer of lace for protection. Did she dare play this out and see where it went?

"I don't think I do." She looked over her shoulder and stuck her tongue out at him.

His hand come down with a light, but stinging blow on her backside. She glared at him. "You can't do that to me." His eyebrows meshed, but his lips remained upturned. Despite his raised arm, he wasn't serious.

"You're not the boss of me," she taunted childishly.

He yanked her panties down to her knees and placed his left hand on her back, holding her against the seat. His touch was light, if she tried, she could free herself. She knew he'd let her go if she asked him. Confident that this was a game, she mocked him. "Get your hands off me."

She didn't anticipate the smack that landed on her left cheek. Pain radiated through her, followed by a pleasant glow that lodged in her pussy. Yikes, she'd heard that spanking could be fun; she'd never expected it to be like this.

She wiggled her ass, silently daring him to do it again. He obliged with two quick blows, right cheek then left. The strikes were infinitesimally harder than the first, the resulting arousal doubly potent. She grumbled a meaningless complaint.

He obliged by removing her panties and stuffing them in her mouth.

Two more blows followed. Each landing beside the previous ones. He stroked her ass lightly and leaned against her back. "Your ass is beautiful with my handprints on it. And I think you like it."

She shook her head, denying his accusation.

His fingers dipped low and grazed across her soaking wet pussy. "See, you love it, you're dripping with honey. Later, I'm going to lick you until you come. Again, and again. And then, I'm going to fuck you until you scream my name."

She pushed back, trying to get him to stroke her harder. He spanked her again, the moisture on his fingers adding to the sting.

"I like how that looks." His voice was a caress. "Your juices glistening in the sun, making that tight, sexy ass shine." He stroked her lips again, gathering moisture and smearing it on her ass. "So hot, so sexy. So wet." He leaned in, his hair tickling her thigh and his tongue flicking across her clit. "So fucking sexy." His words were hot on her over-sensitized flesh. She thrust back against him, but he was gone.

"Did I give you permission to move?" Three fast swats landed on her bottom. She arched back to reach the last one. "Naughty girl. No more for you if you're enjoying it. Up you get." He grasped her waist and pulled her backward. Her groin bumped against his incredible hardness. "Never mind. Stay there." He placed a restraining hand on her back. His belt buckle rattled, his zipper scraped open. Clothing rustled and the head of his cock nudged against her ass.

"Lift your leg, put one foot on the footrest."

She needed him so badly that she moved without hesitation. She lifted her leg and thrust back against him. His cock scraped against her, running along the seam of her ass. She whimpered in dismay. She didn't want games, she wanted him inside her. He shifted, his cock slipped lower, dragged along her folds and across her clit. Pumping a few times, he teased her clit, edging her closer to orgasm. She muttered through her panty gag.

"No talking." He pulled back and slapped her ass again. She bucked in pleasure, tempting him to enter her, to drive his hard length into her. The tip of his cock slipped in and she tried to push back.

He slapped one ass cheek and then the other before grabbing her hips to hold her still. "This is not a game. This is me, taking you, the way that I want to. You don't get a say. You come when I tell you to, and not a second before. Do you understand me?"

She shook her head and pressed backward, only to be rewarded by two more stinging strokes. "I'm warning you, city girl; on my property, I'm in charge and you do what you're told." In one smooth thrust, he buried himself in her pussy until his balls slammed against her clit.

He twitched his hips and his cock pulsed inside her. So long, so wide, he felt incredible. She pulled forward, intent on riding him. Another smack on the ass and one hand fisted in her hair, tugging backward, pulling her head up and back. "No moving."

She stilled, her pussy clenching and throbbing around his enormous length. He filled her completely. He flexed again, his balls danced against her clit, threatening to send her over the edge.

"Elbows on the seat. Raise yourself up."

She shifted until her elbows were on the seat, her breasts hanging free and heavy. He withdrew slowly, pushed against her, seating his cock fully and cupping her breasts in his hands.

"Soft and slow, or hard and fast?" He asked, slowly withdrawing and squeezing tighter on her nipples as he withdrew. Pain radiated from her breasts to her clit and she clamped down as he drove back into her. "Holy shit, that's tight." He pinched and released, she clenched on demand. He cursed. "Remind me to buy you nipple clamps."

He inched back. Slow and sure. Teasing, tantalizing, driving her insane with need. "What's the matter, do you need to come again?"

She whimpered her ascent.

"Too bad. It's my turn." He tugged and abused her left nipple and toyed with her clit with his other hand. Rubbing, circling, pinching, squeezing as he slowly withdrew from her and slid himself home and stopped pumping.

It was heaven, it was hell, she was so close to orgasm, but he was teasing, making her wait. His dirty talk was as big a turn on as his actions. Her panties stifled her, the taste and smell of her arousal fueled her burning desire. Wouldn't he just start fucking? Hard? And give her the orgasm she needed? She needed to feel his lust, his come spurting inside her. She needed him to lose control and take her without regard for her satisfaction. She wanted him to need her so badly that he lost control.

He pinched her clit and nipple. Pinching one while he released the other. Over and over, without moving his cock. Her insides clenched. She was going to come whether he fucked her or not.

Reaching his long arms under her, he spread her lips with one hand and tapped her clit with the other. "Does that feel good, baby?"

She nodded.

He tapped harder, his cock throbbing inside her, but still not fucking.

"Do you need to come?" She whimpered around her gag.

"Don't move." He spanked her clit harder and harder. "You're so sexy, so hot. I can hardly hold myself back. I want to fuck you. I want to drive into you. I want to pound you so hard you scream my name." He increased the speed of his clit spanking until it matched the speed of his words.

Her body tensed, her pussy clenched. She tried to hold back.

He pulled back and slammed into her. His hands left her pussy and grabbed her tits, pulling and tugging as he slammed into her over and over. She forced the panty gag out of her mouth with her tongue and screamed his name. "Please, Joe! Yes! Please!"

He clamped his hand over her mouth and squeezed her entire breast in his fist and she exploded over the edge, coming and groaning and driving back against him until he shouted her name and drove into her once, twice, and again as he exploded into her.

She resurfaced, draped over the quad, gasping for breath. He was bent over her, his twitching cock buried inside as he trailed kisses along her spine. She wiggled against him and he pulled out. His come dribbled down her thigh. She rolled over and wiggled up onto the seat, pulling him with her. "Jesus," she whispered. "Sweet Jesus. That was amazing."

He chuckled against her cheek. "Yes, it was."

She reached between them and scooped up some of his fluid with her fingers. She brought it to her lips and slurped her fingers clean. "Yummy." His cock twitched against her thigh.

"Damn woman. You're killing me."

"You started it," she teased and kissed him, wrapping her legs around his waist and stroking his back. "I'd love to go again, but I need something to drink. Fetch me that wine."

"Not on your life." He laughed, pulled up his pants, hoisted her up in his arms, and carried her to the blanket.

After guzzling a glass of wine and a bottle of water, she sat on the blanket alongside him, surprised to discover that she wasn't embarrassed by her ardent response to his aggressive play. She'd loved the pain-pleasure of his spankings. Being submissive, even to that minor extent, had been freeing. How decadent to give in and follow his lead, letting him pick and choose what happened, leaving nothing to her but to succumb to pleasure and enjoy. Joe taking what he wanted and her playing along, mindlessly, freed her to feel without consequence.

The fabulous side effect was that she wanted to give him the same treatment. To command him, to tell him what to do, to take her pleasure without regard to his. She was used to give and take all at once; she'd never braved these woods before. Could she do it? Could she take charge and expect him to be submissive? Would he allow it? She'd read about domination and submission, who hadn't these days; reading about it was a far cry from doing it. There was an invisible line that would require incredible determination to cross. Before Joe, sex had been vanilla; nothing more than fucking or lovemaking when she was in a serious relationship, but this sex-play had potential.

He lay stretched out on his back, eyes closed, arms tucked behind his head. A light breeze drifted over them, setting the trees in motion, shifting the shade dancing over his body. Sunlight and shadows drew her attention from one part of his torso to another and then to his unbuttoned fly.

"Are you comfortable like that? With your pants on while I'm naked? It doesn't seem fair." She leaned over pulled off his boots and tugged on his jeans. He lifted his hips and his jeans slid slowly down his thighs, exposing his sculpted abs and tight boxer-briefs.

Damn! They hugged his thighs and abdomen like a lover. Torn between staring at his bulge and revealing it fully, she raked her nails over the fabric and down its length, delighted by his twitching response. She removed his pants, discarding them in a heap at his feet. He lay in his underwear, gloriously exposed without even a hint of indignity or unease. Where did men find self-assurance like that?

She certainly didn't have it. None of her female friends had it. She was sitting here naked, beside his nearly nude body, and despite their earlier enjoyment and his pleasure in her body, she couldn't help worry if she was lacking somehow. Disappointed in herself, she pushed the thought away. She'd come to see Joe and he'd been happy to see her, and judging by the twitching response of his cock to the motions of her fingernails, he was still happy to see her. Good enough! She was going to enjoy this moment without fear and let self-recrimination and doubts come later.

Kneeling beside him, she trailed one hand down each of his legs, tickling and teasing as she went. His muscles bunched and jumped under her touch. She delighted in each motion and how the downy hair on his thighs tickled and scratched lightly as she passed. There was something about a man's body that was appealing, so hard and strong and yet soft and yielding. Muscles sculpted from hard work under a thin layer of hair.

She leaned in and trailed her tongue down his thigh, leaving a moist trail behind. Blowing softly, she cooled the trail until goosebumps rose on his flesh. His hand came down on her shoulder, stilling her motions.

"What's up, cowboy? Don't you like that?" She wiggled upward and flicked her tongue against his bulge. He bucked against her.

"This is supposed to be a picnic, not an all-day sex fest." His grumble was light and without heat.

"Poor baby." She nibbled his hard-on through his underwear. "Are you too tired to play? Do you need a nap?" She laughed lightly at his responding growl. "You lay there and rest and I'll find a way to amuse myself."

Swinging one leg over his body, she straddled his thighs below his groin. Tempted as she was to slide higher and sit directly on that bulge, she restrained herself for the moment and toyed with his nipples.

"What are you doing?"

"Shh. No talking. When I want you to speak, I'll ask your opinion." He opened one eye and spared her a lazy, curious look. "And no looking either." She slid her hand down over his eyes, closing them.

"Bossy little thing, aren't you?"

She tweaked his nipple as punishment for talking out of turn. "Turn about is fair play and this is my game. You get to do what I say, nothing more, nothing less. Nod if you understand." He nodded immediately, a tiny smile quirked up the corners of his mouth.

"Do I amuse you?"

"No, ma'am." The smirk morphed into a full-fledged grin.

She slid forward and bit his nipple in punishment; not hard, just enough bite so he'd feel it. He yelped and grasped her head. Grabbing his wrists, she pushed his arms up over his head. "Oh no you don't," she chided. "No talking, no touching." Leaned over him as she was, her breasts dangled in his face. His tongue lashed out and licked wildly. "And definitely no tonguing." She paused and looked down at him. "Don't make me incapacitate you."

"Fat chance of that happening." His low chuckle rumbled through her.

"No way a little bit of a woman like you could restrain me." He didn't even bother to look at her while he mocked her.

She grabbed her panties and stuffed them into his mouth, then tied her light sweater around his head to secure the lacy bit in place. Next, she looped his T-shirt around his arms and pressed them over his head. He went along with her ridiculous attempt at binding him without complaint. Leaning back, she surveyed her handiwork. Wanting a better view, she stood and circled him. Damn, he looked good like that; tempting and delicious enough to eat. Something was missing. No, not missing—the flaw was that he wore too many clothes. She whipped off his socks and underwear leaving his cock exposed and bobbing eagerly.

"That's better." She stood over him, one foot on either side of his hips. "I like you like this, quiet and obedient." His eyes sparkled and he mumbled something behind the makeshift gag.

She glared down at him. "What part of no talking don't you understand—and no, that's not a question." She lowered herself closer until she was squatting a hair's breadth over his pulsing cock, close enough that she could feel the heat radiating off him. Tipping her pelvis back and then forward, she lowered herself fully onto him, trapping his rigid cock between their bodies, against her core. Shock waves of pleasure and heat flooded through her and she gushed moisture as he throbbed and pulsed against her.

She slid the outside of her pussy up and down the length of his cock, snagging delightfully on her lips and clit. "Mm." She shifted so her knees were on the ground on either side of him, her sensitive flesh grinding against him. Kneeling eased the strain on her legs, making it easier to maneuver.

She cupped her breasts in her hands and looked down at him though half-closed eyes. His gaze was fixed on her hands as if he couldn't look away. She released her breasts and trailed her hands up her arms, reaching for the sky, thrusting her breasts forward, teasing Joe with the full view. His arms lifted toward her and she waggled one finger in a no-you-don't gesture; obediently, he let them drop back over his head.

The desire in his eyes and tense body was almost irresistible, the resulting rush was incredible. A naked cowboy under her, waiting to do her bidding. The question was, what did she want? More fucking, his mouth on her pussy, or his cock down her throat? So many choices; each with their own merit.

A flash of inspiration hit. Shifting deftly, she took his cock inside her aching pussy, sinking down on him and engulfing his length in one smooth stroke. He muttered something through his gag.

"No talking." She clenched around his cock and he groaned. Inching upward, she eased off him until the tip of his cock was barely inside her. Dropping down abruptly, she engulfed him fully and swirled her hips in a small circle, dragging her clit across his pelvis. He twisted under her. "Uh-uh. No moving either. Lay back and take what I give. Or you'll get nothing."

She leapt to her feet, laughing at his bobbing cock, jerking and twitching in the air, blindly seeking her warmth. Joe didn't open his eyes; he lay there, body tense, cock spasming. He was going to let her play; her heart fluttered. "That's the way, cowboy. It's time for the country boy to give in to the city girl." His smile acknowledged her twist of his earlier threats.

Kneeling beside him, she blew on his cock and engulfed the tip with her mouth. Her own sweet flavor overlay his. Dark, musky, salty. Damn, the combination of their essences was delicious. Her jaw stretched to the limit, she lowered herself onto him, consuming as much of his length as she could. He was like molten satin under her flicking tongue. Living, pulsing, twitching, moving, and shifting as she swirled her tongue and sucked him deep, losing herself in the moment and loving every second of it.

Her glance took in his expression, the clenched jaw, eyes squeezed shut, bunched cheek muscles. Oh yeah, he was loving this as much as she was. His lips parted and a gasp escaped, it tickled down her body, fueling the fire burning her alive. Enough of this.

Without warning, she straddled him again, reached under herself to position him and sank onto him with a long circling motion. Up and down. Around and around. She rode him, teasing, tormenting, driving herself wild with lust. He writhed under her, fueling her motions. She let his first upward thrust go unremarked. She lifted in opposition to his second thrust, pulled free of him and returned to her knees at his side.

She laughed at his glare and took him into her mouth again, thwarting his attempts to thrust deeply she backed away and released him until he closed his eyes in defeat. Back and forth she went. He played along with the game, taking her lead, letting her control the ride. She rode him, sucked him, pumped with her hand until she couldn't take it any longer.

She straddled his hips, a hair's breadth away from penetration, until he opened his eyes, his gaze pleading with her. He was glorious. Naked, aroused, his cock glistening in the filtered afternoon light, his eyes begging and his hips pivoting. She could stare at him all day. Well, she could—if she didn't need him so damned badly.

She lowered herself and took him inside her core once more. Pivot, rise, swivel, lower. She ground against him, reaping all possible sensation and pleasure from her ride. This time when he bucked, she allowed it. Giving reign to her passions, she changed her pace, she moved in time with Joe, her hips circling as she went up and down, her pelvis tilting forward and back, the complicated triple motion coming easier than she thought it might. They moved in perfect unison, as if they were made for each other. A butterfly of lightness fluttered into her heart; the tender emotion should have worried her, she was here for a fling, nothing more, but the touch of connection felt strangely right.

"Yes." Her cry rent the air. His hands gripped her hips, stilling her motions and he drove frantically into her, his desperate need drove her over the edge and she peaked seconds before him, shattering in pleasure and floating back to earth in a million beautiful pieces.

Leaning against one another, they finished the wine and opened the picnic basket. Its contents weren't at all what she expected. Thick ham and cheese sandwiches made on fresh buns, chocolate chip cookies, and crisp apples. It was a feast made to nourish and fortify, not seduce. It seemed at odds with their impulsive, transient relationship; the meal felt too comfortable, too homey, and made her long for more.

"That was delicious." She tucked the leftovers and wrappers inside the basket. "I'm so stuffed I might never eat again." She laughed.

"You'll have to. I promised Mom I'd have you stay for supper."

"And, do you always listen to your mother?" She crawled on his lap and nibbled his earlobe.

"Not always, but I've never brought a woman home before."

"You didn't bring me home, I followed you here." It was important that he know that this was her doing; she was here on her terms, not his.

"Technically, yes. I did leave a clue for you to find me. I thought you'd call. Frankly, I'd given up hope, and here you are. Warm and willing in my arms." The arm around her waist tightened as he pulled her closer to kiss her hair.

"It wasn't easy to come. We had some fun, but to follow a stranger home?" She shivered, recalling the excitement and trepidation she'd battled on her journey to the ranch. As confessions went, hers was an understatement and a deeply personal revelation. "I lost track of how many times I looked at your card and picked up the phone and changed my mind about calling."

"You could have called, you should have. I'd have come to the city to meet you. You didn't have to come all this way, though I'm glad you did." He wrapped his arms around her, pulled her close, and nuzzled her neck.

Her doubts resurfaced. Was this what she wanted from him? Random sex with a virtual stranger? Or could they deepen this and discover each other and turn this impulsive meeting into the realm of friendship, or something more?

"What?" he asked. "You went all stiff in my arms. What are you thinking?"

"Nothing. It's okay, just random thoughts." Hoping to end the discussion, she leaned in and kissed him again.

"Why don't we take a walk? There's a beautiful meadow down that path and you haven't even been to the water yet. There's a swimming hole. The water's chilly, but on warm summer days it's perfect for swimming."

He pressed a quick kiss to her forehead. "Come on, city girl. Let's take a walk." With a quick rolling motion, he flipped them over so she was laying half under him, his body pressing her gently into the ground. "I'd love to make love to you again, but that's not all I'm about. I want to know *who* you are too."

His gaze caught hers; she was tempted to look away. How could she be disappointed that he wanted to walk, not have sex, when learning more about him was exactly what she'd been thinking? Damn her fickle brain and traitorous body. He felt so damned good against him, she was tempted to seduce him again.

"A walk it is." She wiggled out from beneath him and slipped into her clothing.

"You didn't have to get dressed." He leered and waggled his eyebrows as he pulled his jeans on.

"Yes, I did. Otherwise, you'd just distract me, and the walk would be short-lived. Besides, you've got staff and who knows when someone will show up?" God, even the thought was mortifying. It hadn't even occurred to her while they were busy exploring each other. He made her forget her rules and her surroundings. She was going to have to get creative and figure out how to disentangle herself from his mesmerizing presence if she intended to get to know him better.

"Come on, let's walk along the creek." He held out his hand.

She took his work roughened hand in hers for a moment and released it to walk beside him. His touch was too electric to maintain contact and keep her distance. If this was going to be about getting to know each other, she'd have to ensure they kept a minimum physical distance between them because every time he touched her, even the most casual brushing of his fingers or arm against her, passion and need exploded over her and she forgot where she was. The sex was good, hell, it was great, but the connection they seemed to have forged so long ago at Gina's was what she wanted to explore. Could they build a friendship, a serious relationship, or was sex, admittedly fabulous earth-shaking sex, all that was destined to be between them?

"Where are you?"

She glanced around, Joe was four or five steps ahead of her. "Sorry, I was thinking. Apparently, I can't think and walk at the same time. Kind of like patting my head and rubbing my tummy."

"Deep thoughts?" His brows furrowed. "Regrets already?"

"Too deep for a beautiful day like this." She whirled around taking in the bright sunshine, the beautiful trees, and the trickling stream. "But no, not regrets. Just unanswered questions. Questions I won't let mar this lovely afternoon." She walked past him, shoulder bumping him playfully on her way by. "Tell me something about Joe Brooks; what makes him tick?"

"Okay, on one condition." He grabbed her hand from behind. "Stop moving away; hold my hand and let's walk together. I like touching you."

"And if I deny your request?" She grinned as he caught up to her. Half of her wanted him to agree to let her walk alone; the other traitorous half, wanted him to insist on holding hands. They walked in silence for a moment, their footsteps soundless on the plush grass along the creek bank.

"If you deny me, I'll talk anyway. But, I am curious, you've got this whole come close and take a nibble then back away thing going on. I don't understand it. Is this a game?"

Damn. She'd hoped he wouldn't notice her waffling back and forth between curiosity and unbridled desire. Crap and double crap. She sucked at keeping her feelings hidden.

"I'm not doing it on purpose. Okay, I am. But not really." She floundered to a stop, her feet matching the halting of her brain. She stood staring at him, unsure how to clarify her thoughts.

"Well, that clears things right up." He laughed and kissed her knuckles.

"Look, I came here today because I thought we connected at Buffalo Days. I mean, we had this incredible sex." She ignored the heat rising in her cheeks and focused her gaze on his face. "Really great sex, but afterward, when we sat and talked, we seemed to, I don't know, we seemed to connect. I came here to see if that connection was real or if I'd imagined it. But one look at you and all I could think about was getting my hands on you." Dear God, would the earth just split and swallow her alive? Now would be good.

"Oh, thank Christ." He laughed and tugged her into his embrace. He kissed her on the forehead and wrapped his arm around her shoulders, propelling her forward on the path. "I was beginning to think this was all sex for you. Not that I mind sex, because damn! But, when we talked for so long, so easily,

I wondered if this could be more. That's why I slipped my card into your pocket that night. Although, I admit, my dick is making it hard to hold a conversation right now. I want you again."

She laughed at the red flush staining his cheeks. A cowboy who blushed. Hot damn, if that didn't amp up his appeal ten-fold. She leaned her head against his chest, loving the way his arm dropped to her waist to tug her even closer. They walked until they rounded a corner to a pile of boulders set in the curve of the creek.

"Wow. It's lovely." She scampered up to the top of the pile and settled down to enjoy the view. Sitting twenty feet up, she could see for miles. A splash turned her attention to the creek. A fish jumped in a deep pool, its scales glistening in the sun. Across the creek, cattle roamed fields near and far, some so distant they were nothing more than dark specks on a field of green. "Is that all yours?" She nodded to the open fields across the stream, stretching for as far as she could see.

"No. But my land, my family's land, does stretch out a few miles."

"Cool. I can't even fathom the vastness out here. I've lived in the city for so long, in my teeny tiny one-bedroom apartment, that this…this space is awe-inspiring." She gestured widely, encompassing everything she saw.

"I've lived here my whole life, except for university, and it still awes me." He scrambled up to sit beside her, almost, but not quite touching. "Look over there." He gestured to the west. "That's a hawk. I can't tell what kind from here. But watch how it circles and soars, searching for prey."

She watched in awe for several minutes until it swooped down, dive bombing the ground only to soar upwards again with something small dangling from its claws.

"Ouch." She laughed at herself. "Yup, city girl here. That was harsh but so impressive. I've never seen anything like that before."

"You miss a lot living in the city. It's a different world out here. Come on, there's a lot more to see."

Back on the quad, they toured vast fields of cattle. She watched him check on a calf he claimed was newly delivered. He proclaimed it safe and healthy, but noted its position so he could send someone out to tag it. Most of the ranch's birthing was done early in spring, but there were always a few late catches to watch for. His barns were enormous. Six barns stood in line like pristine red and white soldiers. Not traditional barns. But fabricated steel buildings with the latest and greatest in technology, lighting, and ventilation. There were numerous small sheds and outbuildings, chicken coops, pig pens, and even a rabbit hutch.

She shed a few tears when he told her the rabbits weren't pets, but rather were for food along with the chickens, turkeys, and pigs. They didn't eat the goats, who were raised for milk and cheese

"That's about it." He grinned over his shoulder at her. "There's more, but I won't bore you. My family built this place from a small homestead. I think I'll always be happy here."

"It's enormous." She climbed off the quad when they returned to the house. "How do you keep it up like this?"

"It's a family business. My brothers and I look after it together. The four of us are equal partners, and we have a shit-ton of staff."

"But it's named the Joe Brooks Cattle Company." She squinted up at him when he chuckled.

"After my great-grandfather, grandfather, and father. Technically, I'm the fourth Joe Brooks."

"Doesn't that bother your brothers?"

"Not-" His mother's voice interrupted his reply.

"Joseph Brooks, you get your butt in here now. I've been holding dinner for you and your guest and your brothers are famished." His mother stood on the porch, one hand on her hip, the other shaking her finger at him. "And turn your phone back on." She pivoted on her heel and disappeared into the house, the screen door slamming behind her for emphasis.

"Nope, my brothers don't mind. Ma rules the roost around here." He laughed.

Dinner was a riotous affair with lots of good-natured teasing and joking. Joe's brothers rode him relentlessly for having a girlfriend, despite two of them being married with kids of their own. His sister-in-laws were friendly and welcoming, even if they did caution Alex that Joe wasn't one to date much and never more than a few times. They claimed he wasn't a man-whore, just picky. The idea didn't bother her much, she'd guessed that about him already. He was entirely too good-looking to be dateless, and he'd mentioned not bringing any other women home.

"And that is my family." He declared as they walked to her car. "My mom, three brothers, two sister-in-laws, two nieces, three nephews. I've got half a dozen aunts and uncles and a wagon-full of cousins; thankfully they weren't here."

"They were a lot of fun. A bit overwhelming, but fun."

"And your family?"

"Just my sister and I. My folks died a few years ago. Not too many cousins."

"Good. That means they won't be around to interfere with me calling on you."

"And will you be calling on me?" She teased, passing her lips quickly across his.

"Hell yes."

"You don't have my number."

"Then I'll have to kiss it out of you." He swooped in, drawing her into his embrace. His lips brushed across hers, warm and welcoming in the cool evening air.

Goosebumps rose over her skin and she leaned into him, absorbing his enticing heat. Around his family, she'd barely been able to bank her desire for him, and now with her body pressed full length against his, it blossomed anew, heat and desire consuming her. She pressed against him, his rock-hard cock heaven against her. Her fingers tangled in his hair, yanking his head down closer. She devoured his mouth, tasting, exploring, learning him anew.

Her arms slid around his waist, fingers tracing the sleek lines of his muscles, navigating the plains of his back. She yanked his t-shirt from his belt, and slid her hands up his back.

Joe groaned into her mouth. She was fucking killing him. She was so hot, so sexy, he wanted her again. Here. Now. He grabbed her ass and hoisted her up, turning to place her on the trunk of her car. She smelled like heaven, not perfume, but natural woman mixed with his mom's good cooking. A man could lose himself in scent alone, but her body? He'd never get enough of her body. He kissed his way down her neck and across the top of her shirt. Her nipples pebbled against his palms when he cupped her breast. Following her lead, he pulled her shirt up and bent to take a single, perfect nipple into his mouth. Her shiver and groan of delight were like music to his body. His cock throbbed and pulsed, begging to be buried inside her.

A shrill whistle sounded and he jerked back.

"Get a freaking room, bro."

"Screw you." He shouted back and leaned back in, his tongue flicking across the rigid peak of her breast.

"Joe?" Her soft voice pulled him out of his fantasy world and he tugged her shirt back into place and leaned his head against hers.

"Sorry, Alex. You make me forget where I am."

She chuckled. "Yeah, me too. But I better go. It's a long drive and it's already late."

"I could drive you home." He offered hopefully.

"And what about my car? And where would you stay? I'm not ready to have you over yet. It's too soon."

The vulnerability in her voice didn't surprise him. She was brazen, bold and sexy, but beneath it all, she was a touch shy and reserved. It had taken months for her to seek him out. While their bodies might be in perfect sync, her mind wasn't caught up yet. He suspected that might take a while.

"Fine. Be mean to me." He brushed his lips over hers. She leaned into him, deepening the kiss, and in seconds, they were both breathless. "Come on, city girl. Into the car. Off you go. Text me when you get home."

Several long slow kisses later, she pushed him aside and slid off the car. "Goodnight, Joe. Sleep well."

"No chance of that, not with this hard-on. My dick's like a fence post."

"Take a shower, deal with it." She winked and climbed into the car.

"Give me your phone and I'll give you my cell number. Text when you get home." His fingers danced over the screen before he handed the phone back.

"Sexy Rancher?" She asked with a laugh when she looked at his entry.

"You better believe it, and don't forget to text when you're safe." He leaned in and kissed her lightly on the cheek. She fired up the car and in moments her tail lights disappeared from sight.

Safely curled up in her bed, Alex sent Joe a text. *Home safe. Thanks for everything.*

I wish I was in bed with you. He responded.

She sent back: *Don't even start that.*

So, no sexting then? He sent back with a leering emoji.

Not tonight. I had a good time today. Thank you. She sent along a kissy face.

Me too. I'm glad you came out. Sleep well, city girl.

You too, rancher. She followed it up with a row of Z's.

She'd barely set the phone down on the nightstand when it vibrated. He'd sent a glass of wine and a daisy.

She set the phone back down. She wasn't going to answer him or this would go on all night. She'd contact him in a few days. No sense seeming too eager. She snuggled under the covers with a smile; today hadn't gone the way she'd expected. She showed up looking to get to know him better, but somehow, he'd managed to distract her with an afternoon of wickedly good sex and tricked her into meeting his family. She should have felt cornered, but she didn't. She felt welcome and she wasn't sure what she thought about that.

Time would tell, because she did want to see him again. She needed another taste of that delectable body: those hard abs, his gloriously muscled back, and that ass. Sweet heaven, the man had the nicest ass she'd ever seen.

Her fingers traced their way over her breasts, down her abdomen, and into the juncture of her thighs. Oh yeah, she was hot and wet already. Damn, he had the hottest effect on her body. She swirled three fingers in slow circles over her clit until orgasm exploded over her. Temporarily sated, she drifted into sleep thinking of his smile and wondering what would happen on their first *real* date.

Other Books by Katie

Erotic Romance/ Erotic

Stand Alone Titles

Tessa's Trio
The Gift

Covet the Cowboy Series

Corralling the Cowboy (Book 1)
Cornering the Cowgirl (Book 2)

Contemporary Romance Series

Heart's Haven (Resplendence Publishing)
Running Home
Saving Grace
Building Trust

Contemporary Romance Single Title

To a Tea
Rekindled Fire

About Katie O'Connor

Katie O'Connor lives in Calgary, Alberta, Canada. She married her high school sweetheart and is living her happily ever after. She is the mother of two grown daughters and is extremely proud of her five grandchildren. She has two wonderful sons-in-law and a large support network of friends, family and fellow authors.

Katie's career path has been long and twisted, with most of her life devoted to her family. She's been a waitress, chambermaid, cashier, store manager, as well as a lab and x-ray technician. She is an avid quilter and crafter

She's dabbled in writing since high school because something drives her to create stories. She swears that it's impossible for her NOT to write. She says, "I think my head would explode if I kept all those ideas trapped inside. I even dream story lines. My mind is a wildly creative place and all those ideas have to be downloaded to relieve the pressure."

She believes in all things magical including dragons, fairies, UFOs, ghosts, and house pixies. But most of all she believes in love, romance and hope.

Katie likes to make it up as she goes along and dreams of publishing a mixed genre novel. It is going to be an erotic, shape shifter, vampire, steampunk, sci-fi, murder mystery, adventure, romantic, western, historical, thriller. It will be her biography.

Contact Katie O' Connor

Katie loves to hear from her readers. Feel free to contact her anytime.

Website: https://katieohwrites.com
Email: katieoconnorwrites@gmail.com
Facebook: http://www.facebook.com/katieohwrites

Reviews are an authors life blood.
To thank readers generous enough to leave a review, I am holding month draw for a free e-book of the reviewers choosing.
To enter, simply email me the link to your review.

www.ingramcontent.com/pod-product-compliance
Lightning Source LLC
Chambersburg PA
CBHW071518030726

47593CB00003B/1314